NOW YOU CAN READ...
Aladdin

STORY ADAPTED BY LUCY KINCAID

ILLUSTRATED BY ERIC KINCAID

BRIMAX BOOKS · NEWMARKET · ENGLAND

Once there was a magician. He went to China to look for a magic lamp. The lamp was in a cave. The way  into the cave was along a tunnel. To touch the walls of the tunnel meant certain death. The magician wanted the lamp but he was afraid to go along the tunnel.

"I will ask someone else to get the lamp for me," said the magician.

He asked a boy called Aladdin.
The magician did not tell Aladdin
he would die if he touched the
walls of the tunnel.
Aladdin said he would get the lamp.

Aladdin was ready to go.

The magician gave him a ring.

"Wear this," said the magician.

"It will keep you safe."

"Safe from what?" asked Aladdin.

"Er . . . nothing," said the magician.

"You will find the lamp at the back of the cave."

Aladdin was away for a long time.
"He must have touched the walls of
the tunnel. He must be dead," said
the magician. Then he saw Aladdin
coming back.
"Give me the lamp,"
said the magician.
Aladdin put the
lamp up his sleeve.
"Help me out of
the tunnel first,"
he said.

"Give me the lamp," said the magician. "Then I will help you out of the tunnel."

Aladdin did not trust the magician. "No!" he said. "Help me out first."

The magician became angry. "If you will not give me the lamp you can stay there forever!" he said.

Then he closed the mouth of the tunnel with a magic spell.

Aladdin was trapped. He did not know what to do. By chance he rubbed the ring on his finger. There was a puff of smoke. A genie appeared.

"Who are you? What do you want?" asked Aladdin.

"I am the Genie of the Ring. Your wish is my command," said the genie.

"Then take me home," said Aladdin.

Suddenly Aladdin was at home. He did not know how he had got there. The lamp was still up his sleeve. "We can sell this and buy food," he said.
"I will clean it first," said his mother.

Aladdin's mother rubbed at the lamp. There was a puff of smoke. A genie appeared.

Aladdin's mother was afraid. She hid her face.
Aladdin was not afraid. "Who are you?" he asked.
"I am the Genie of the Lamp," said the genie. "Your wish is my command."

The genie gave Aladdin everything he asked for.

Time went by. Aladdin had fine clothes to wear. He lived in a palace. He had a princess for a wife.

One day Aladdin went hunting. The princess was in the palace alone. She heard a pedlar calling. "New lamps for old!" he cried. "I will change Aladdin's old lamp for a new one," said the princess. Aladdin had not told her it was a magic lamp.

She took the lamp and gave it to the pedlar. The pedlar had the lamp in his hand. He threw off his ragged coat. The pedlar was really the magician.

"Now everything
Aladdin has shall
be mine," he said.
He rubbed the magic
lamp.
"What is your
command, master?"
asked the Genie of
the Lamp.
"Take the princess,
myself, the palace
and everything
in it to Africa,"
said the magician.
The genie had to
obey the command.

Aladdin came home. There was
nothing where the palace had been.
Aladdin guessed what had happened.
He rubbed the magic ring.
"What is your command, master?"
asked the Genie of the Ring.
"Bring back my princess and my
palace!" said Aladdin.
"Only the Genie of the Lamp can do
that, master."
"Then take me to my princess,"
said Aladdin.

The princess was glad to see Aladdin. "Where is the magic lamp?" asked Aladdin.

"The magician has it up his sleeve," said the princess.

"Put this powder in his wine," said Aladdin. "It will make him sleep."

The princess did as Aladdin asked.

When the magician was asleep, Aladdin took the lamp. The princess was afraid the magician would wake up. "Please be careful," she said.

Aladdin rubbed the lamp with his sleeve. The genie appeared.

"What is your command, master?" asked the genie.

"Take the palace and everyone in it back to China. But leave the magician here in Africa," said Aladdin.

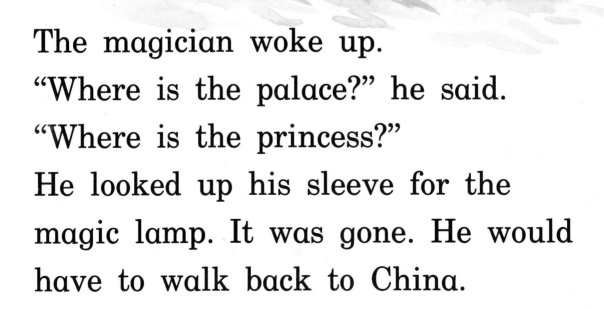

The magician woke up.
"Where is the palace?" he said.
"Where is the princess?"
He looked up his sleeve for the
magic lamp. It was gone. He would
have to walk back to China.

The magician never did get back
to China. Aladdin and his princess
lived happily ever after.

All these appear in the pages of
the story. Can you find them?

magician

Aladdin

tunnel   lamp